THE TALE OF

By Shalini Vallepur

Minneapolis, Minnesota

Credits
All images are courtesy of Shutterstock.com, unless otherwise specified.
With thanks to Getty Images, Thinkstock Photo and iStockphoto.

Front Cover – Aleksandra Novakovic, artphotoclub, kzww, panotthorn, OlgaTik, caramelina, picoStudio, asantosg. Recurring images - Aleksandra Novakovic, artphotoclub, kzww, panotthorn, OlgaTik, caramelina, picoStudio, asantosg, Cool Vector Make, Viktorija Reuta, VectorShow. 2&3 - olllikeballoon. 4&5 - Incomible, pikepicture. 6&7 - Jen Watson, kid315, BLAGORODEZ. 8&9 - Hari Mahidhar, javarman. 10&11 - Karen.T, Anjadora, BLAGORODEZ. 12&13 - Hung Chung Chih, TRphotos. 14&15 - brgfx, peacefoo, ProStockStudio, Vladimir Zhoga, Aurora72, Domenic Toretto, Inspiring. 16&17 - brgfx, domnitsky, muklis setiawan, ProStockStudio, Vorontsova Anastasiia, Aurora72, Domenic Toretto. 18&19 - AnnaTamila, aphotostory, Lukiyanova Natalia frenta, norikko, Phattana Stock, YURY TARANIK, AlexeiLogvinovich. 20&21 - DronaVision, Elena Veselova, gowithstock, Irina Burakova, TZIDO SUN, Irina Burakova, Natalia Aggiato. 22&23 - Chubarov Alexandr, domnitsky, Naida Jazmin Ochoa, Siberian Art, VectorShow.

Library of Congress Cataloging-in-Publication Data

Names: Vallepur, Shalini, author.
Title: The tale of tea / by Shalini Vallepur.
Description: Fusion edition. | Minneapolis, MN : Bearport Publishing Company, [2021] | Series: Drive thru | Includes bibliographical references and index.
Identifiers: LCCN 2020010630 (print) | LCCN 2020010631 (ebook) | ISBN 9781647473266 (library binding) | ISBN 9781647473310 (paperback) | ISBN 9781647473365 (ebook)
Subjects: LCSH: Tea–Juvenile literature.
Classification: LCC SB271 .V35 2021 (print) | LCC SB271 (ebook) | DDC 633.7/2–dc23
LC record available at https://lccn.loc.gov/2020010630
LC ebook record available at https://lccn.loc.gov/2020010631

For more information, write to Bearport Publishing, 5357 Penn Avenue South, Minneapolis, MN 55419. Printed in the United States of America.

CONTENTS

Hop in the Teapot 4
The Tale of Tea 6
Perfect Weather 8
A Tea Plantation 10
The Harvest 12
To the Factory 14
Bag It Up! 16
A World of Tea 18
Time for Tea! 22
Glossary 24
Index 24

HOP IN THE TEAPOT

Hello! I'm Rani, and this is my food truck. It is called the Teapot because I serve the best tea around. Which tea do you want to try?

*** MENU ***

Black tea

Green tea

White tea

Oolong tea

Oh, no! I've run out of tea. I need to get more. Hop in the Teapot, and I'll tell you the tale of tea.
THE TEAPOT

THE TALE OF TEA

Tea is grown around the world. It is grown on farms called **plantations.**

China, India, Sri Lanka, and Kenya grow the most tea in the world.

Tea comes from leaves that grow on small bushes. The leaves are green and shiny.

PERFECT WEATHER

Tea grows best in places that are warm and get a lot of rain.

This tea map shows some of the places where tea is grown.

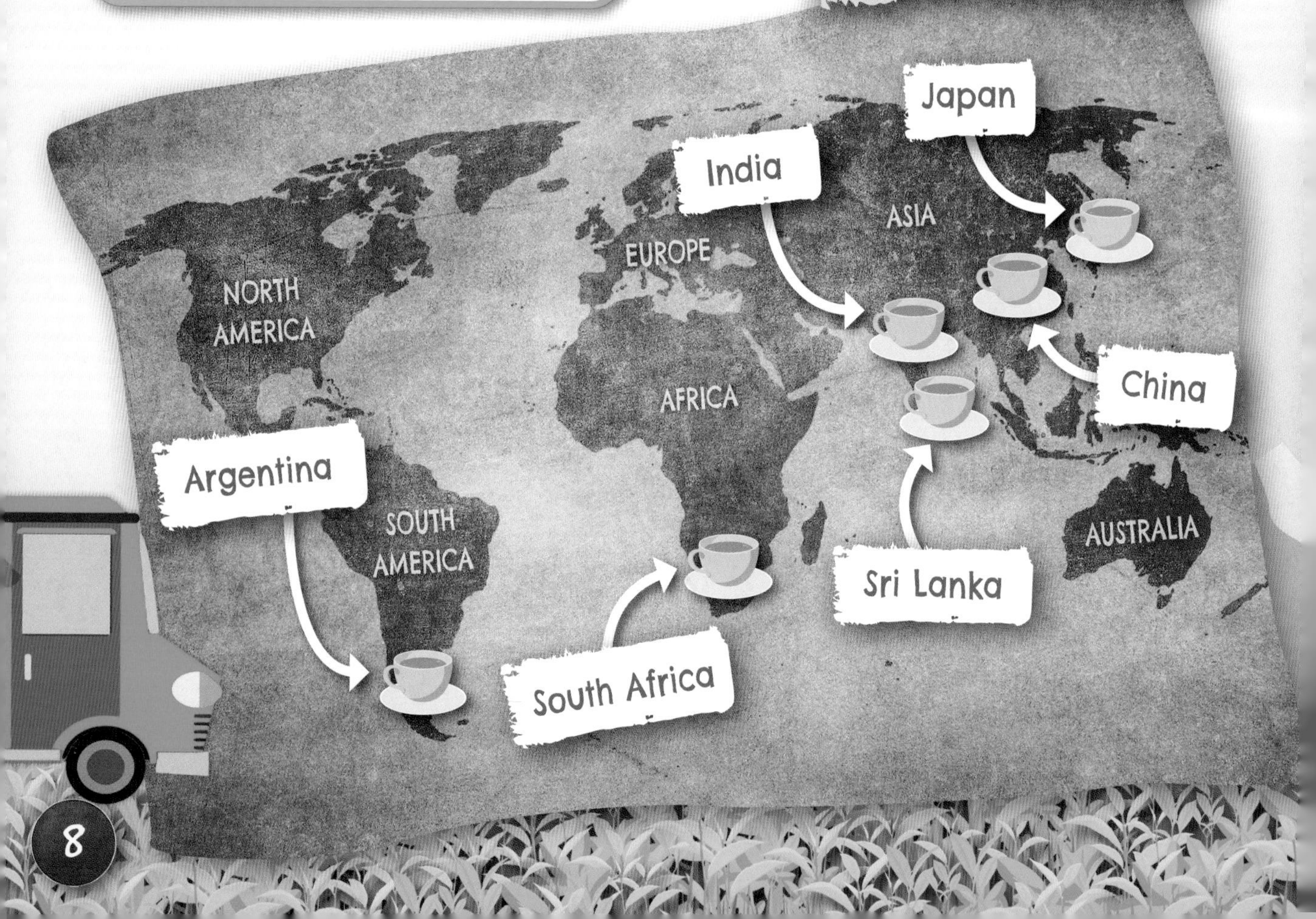

Japan

India

ASIA

EUROPE

NORTH AMERICA

AFRICA

China

Argentina

SOUTH AMERICA

AUSTRALIA

Sri Lanka

South Africa

Tea plantation
in Assam, India
The **soil** that tea grows in is very important. The soil affects how the tea grows and how it will taste.
Teas can be named after the places where they are grown, such as Assam and Darjeeling.

A TEA PLANTATION

We made it to the tea plantation! The leaves are ready to be **harvested** when the bushes reach about 3 feet (1 m) tall.

Some tea plantations have houses and schools for the workers and their families. A lot of tea is grown on smaller farms.

THE HARVEST

Workers pick off the buds and two or three leaves from the top of each stem. Only a few leaves are taken from each bush so the bush keeps growing.

Workers come back after a week to harvest again.

The harvested leaves are placed in baskets and then taken to the factory.
Big machines are sometimes used to harvest leaves, but the best tea comes from handpicked leaves.
THE TEAPOT

TO THE FACTORY

The harvested tea leaves are brought to a factory. The leaves are left to dry for about 12–18 hours.

Once they are dry, the leaves can be rolled by hand or in a big machine. After this, the rolled leaves are put on tables to **ferment.**

Green teas do not ferment for very long. Black teas ferment for a long time.

BAG IT UP!

After tea is fermented, some types of tea need to be baked to make sure they are ready to drink. After this, the tea is **packaged** and sold!

Black tea

Look at how much the tea leaf has changed.

Some companies sell tea as it is. This is called loose leaf tea. A lot of companies put the tea into little bags called tea bags.

A WORLD OF TEA

Tea was first enjoyed around 5,000 years ago in China. Now it is one of the most popular drinks in the world.

Let's take a look at some of the tasty ways that people enjoy tea!

A green tea called matcha is served during tea **ceremonies** in Japan.

MATCHA

MASALA CHAI

Masala chai is a tea from India. Hot tea is mixed with milk and spices.

Iced tea comes from the U.S. It is cold and sweet—perfect on a hot summer's day!

ICED TEA

Bubble tea is a drink from Taiwan. It is sweet, milky, and has little **tapioca** balls floating in it.

BUBBLE TEA

HERBAL TEA

Herbal teas can be made from the flowers, leaves, and roots of different kinds of plants such as mint and raspberry.

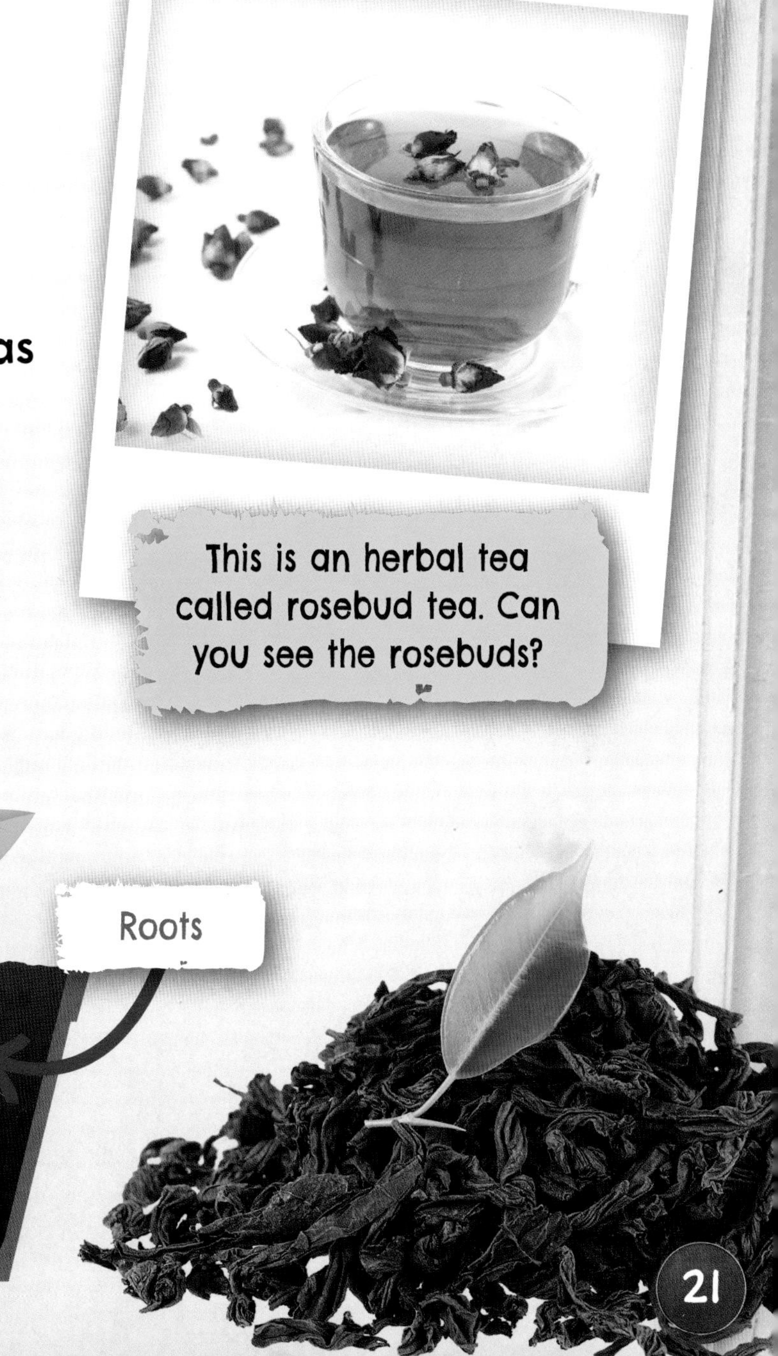

This is an herbal tea called rosebud tea. Can you see the rosebuds?

TIME FOR TEA!

Now we know the tale of tea, and we have lots of tasty types to try. I'm going to make some. Which tea would you like?

* MENU *

Black tea

Green tea

White tea

Oolong tea

Did you know that tea is good for you? Tea is full of **antioxidants** that keep our bodies healthy. So, drink up!
GREEN TEA
20 Tea bags

GLOSSARY

antioxidants tiny things that are good for us and can be found in food and drinks

ceremonies formal occasions celebrating things such as achievements, people, or religious events

ferment when food breaks down and changes on the inside

harvested when fully grown crops have been picked

packaged placed into a wrapping or container

plantations areas of land where crops such as tea are grown

soil the top layer of land that plants can grow in

tapioca a type of food that is used in teas and puddings

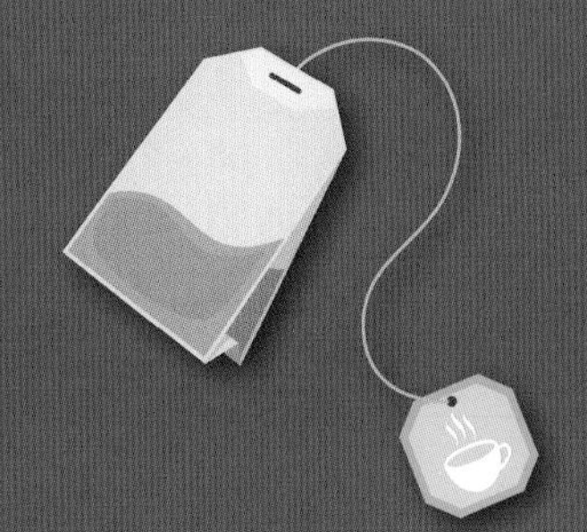

INDEX

factories 13–14

machines 13, 15

milk 19–20

plantations 6–7, 9–11

tea bags 17

tea plant 7, 21